Pip and Posy

www.worldofpipandposy.com

First published 2012 by Nosy Crow Ltd
This paperback edition first published 2014
The Crow's Nest, 10a Lant Street
London SE1 1QR
www.nosycrow.com

ISBN 978 0 85763 144 2

Nosy Crow and associated logos are trademarks and/or registered
trademarks of Nosy Crow Ltd
Text copyright © Nosy Crow 2012
Illustration copyright © Axel Scheffler 2012

The right of Axel Scheffler to be identified as the illustrator
of this work has been asserted.

A CIP catalogue record for this book is available from the British Library.

Printed in China

1 3 5 7 9 8 6 4 2

Pip and Posy

The Big Balloon

Axel Scheffler

nosy
crow

Pip had a balloon.
A balloon of his very own.
It was big and red and round,
and Pip liked it very much indeed.

Pip took it to show Posy.
She thought it was a lovely balloon too.
They decided to take it for a walk.

Everyone who looked at
the balloon smiled.

It made people happy to see it.

But then, by mistake,
Pip let the balloon go!

The balloon floated
into the air.

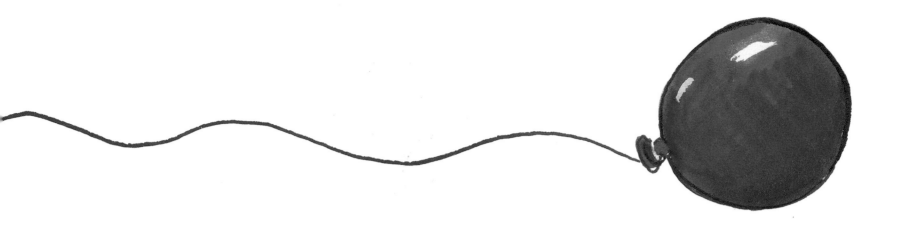

Pip and Posy chased the balloon.

But it floated
higher . . .

And then,
BANG!
It popped!

Oh dear!

Pip was very, very sad that
the balloon had burst.

He cried . . .

and cried . . .

and cried.

Poor Pip!

Then Posy had a really
good idea.

She said that they should
blow bubbles.

ALL the bubbles floated away.

And ALL the
bubbles popped.

But Pip and Posy didn't mind, because
that's what bubbles are supposed to do!

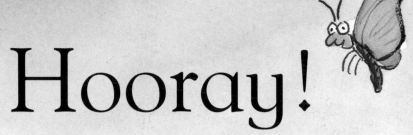

Hooray!